Cody and Grandpa's Christmas Tradition

Gary Metivier • Illustrated by Traci Van Wagoner

PELICAN PUBLISHING COMPANY
GRETNA 2016

ISBN: 9781455621705
E-book ISBN: 9781455621712

Printed in Malaysia
Published by Pelican Publishing Company, Inc.
1000 Burmaster Street, Gretna, Louisiana 70053

To those who can't be there to celebrate traditions but are certainly there in spirit in our hearts. —G. M.
Thanks for your service, Dad. And thanks, Mom and Dad, for all the family traditions. —T. V.

Ding Dong.

Cody and his Chihuahua, Charlie, spring off the couch. They are the official greeters.

Mom and Dad are getting food ready, and Grandpa is still upstairs in his room. Cody straightens his new bow tie and pulls the front door open.

Brrrrr. The cold air grabs at his face like a monster claw.

Shuffle, shuffle. Step, step. Squeak, squeak.
One by one, the Christmas Eve party guests
scurry in.

Swish. Uncle Bob slides past with a pat on the
tippy top of Cody's head and a platter full of
meat and cheese.

Wobble, wobble. Aunt Pam giggles past juggling jiggling plates of Jell-O.

"Pies in the sky!" Great-Aunt Louise holds her prized pies up high.

"Are they apple pies? Cherry?" Cody asks. But he knows the answer already.

She waves them under his nose. "They are meat pies, silly. We have them every year. It's a tradition."

Cody wrinkles his nose. "I want to know who made pie with meat in it a tradition," he whispers to Charlie. "Gross."

But Cody has a problem bigger than meat pies.
Everyone is here now, talking and laughing.
Everyone but Grandpa. Cody's parents told him
Grandpa likes his own time on Christmas Eve.

Cody looks at the clock. *Tick tock.* 10 o'clock. Still no Grandpa.

Tick tock. 11 o'clock.

Tick tock. It's thirty minutes until midnight. Still no Grandpa.

The party is almost over. Christmas is almost here.

"Charlie," Cody says, "we have to check on Grandpa."

Swoosh! Cody runs up the stairs, two steps at a time. Charlie's little legs struggle to keep up.

Grandpa is in his big stuffed chair, facing the window. He is holding an old picture.

"Are you coming down for Christmas, Grandpa?" Cody asks.

Pat! Pat! Grandpa slaps his lap.

Cody climbs up. Charlie jumps up too. He licks Grandpa's face.

"Who are those guys in the picture?" Cody asks.

"No one has ever asked me about this picture," Grandpa says, tugging on Cody's bow tie. "But if you really want to know . . ."

"I do!" Cody insists. "Charlie does too."

Grandpa rubs Charlie's little belly until his hind legs shake.

"Well, all right then. It seems like a good night to share a story."

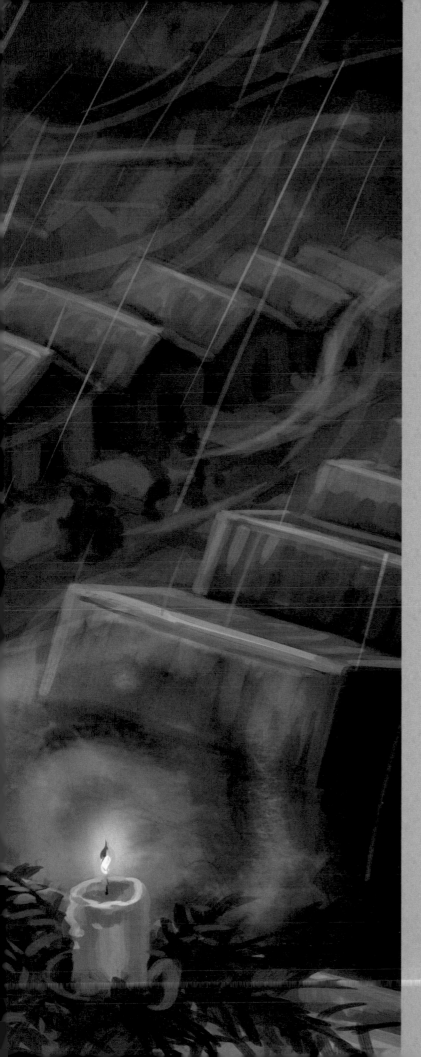

It was on this night a long time ago. I had to be far away from my family on Christmas.

I was a soldier in a place called Vietnam. Members of my unit were sitting on our beds in our hootches. Hootches are like barracks, big rooms full of bunk beds. The walls were made of thin wood and the rooftops were tin. When the rain came down it would clatter so hard you could hardly hear the people inside talking.

Plink! Plink! Plink!

The wind would wail right through the cracks.

Howl!

Strong gusts would pound on the sides like someone beating a drum.

Boom! Boom! Boom!

It was just about midnight on Christmas Eve. The winds were still. No plinks. No howls. No booms. Six of us were sharing our letters and pictures and really missing our families. My best friend, Dale, came running in.

"There is a really bright star out there," he shouted. "It's so bright I bet our families can see it shining too. Let's be under the same star as they are tonight."

We walked out and gazed up at the sky. First five men, then ten, and soon all of the men from all of the hootches silently walked out to join us. No one said a word at first. Then, at exactly midnight, one man started to sing "Silent Night." Someone else joined in. Then another.

Soon hundreds of soldiers were singing together under that bright star. When the song was over, some traded hugs, others handshakes, some pats on the back—but it was silent again. Words weren't needed. We all knew that would always be our special Christmas in Vietnam.

Cody wipes away Grandpa's tears.

"That sounds cool," Cody says. "But why does it make you sad?"

"Because it was the last time many of us would ever be together."

"But you still remember them?"

"I will never forget them. Before we left Vietnam, all of the guys in this picture promised to try to find our star on Christmas Eve. We would start a Christmas tradition to think about each other and those who didn't come home. That's why I sit here and look at the sky at midnight. But I can't see the star from here tonight. The clouds are in the way."

Cody turned to the cuckoo clock on the wall. It is five minutes until midnight. He looks out the window.

"I have an idea!" Cody exclaims. "Are you allowed to share your star?"

"You bet," Grandpa answers.

Cody jumps up and rushes downstairs. Charlie
is right at his heels.

"Everybody outside!" Cody hollers.

"Okay, Grandpa, we are ready," he shouts
upstairs.

Hand in hand, they walk out the front door.
The cold air stings. Cody tucks Charlie in his
coat. Only his head is sticking out.

"We can all remember your friends together.
Then Christmas Eve won't be so sad anymore.
It'll be our new tradition, if that's okay
with you."

"It's better than okay."

The cold wind blows the clouds back and forth.
Just at midnight, a sparkle comes through the
clouds as they slowly pull apart.

"Wow!" Cody points. "That's the brightest star
I have ever seen."

Grandpa starts singing. "Silent night. Holy
night."

Cody's parents start singing too. "All is calm.
All is bright."

Everyone else joins in. Charlie howls. Howling
is the closest he can get to singing.

Grandpa puts his arm around Cody. "Thank you. This is the best present ever."

Cody smiles. "Maybe traditions aren't that bad after all. I might even try a little piece of that meat pie this year."

"Woof!" Charlie agrees.

AUTHOR'S NOTE

Some of my favorite childhood memories involve Christmas traditions. And yes, one of them was meat pies!

My mom would spend an entire day baking made-from-scratch meat pies just like her mother and her grandmother before her.

Team that with another tradition and you'll see why I wrote this book. When I was a boy, all of my brothers and sisters would come home for Christmas. And when I say "all," I mean my six brothers and five sisters! One Christmas, one of my brothers could not make it home. Keith was stationed in Guam serving our country. In our family, we had a buddy system where older siblings teamed up with the younger ones; Keith and I were buddies. One by one, the out-of-town siblings came in by car and plane. But my buddy was not there. And no matter how hard I tried, that Christmas was not the same. He was home the next year, and the year after, until, years later, some of us started our own families and started our own traditions.

For those of you who are missing your traditions this year, missing someone you have lost, or missing someone who just can't be home, think about starting a new tradition—even if it is just sitting around the tree in the quiet of Christmas night thinking about the wonderful times you have enjoyed. And maybe, just maybe, try a piece of meat pie.